Trouble for Letang and Julie

By Beverley Naidoo
Illustrated by Petra Röhr–Rouendaal

Class 3M's new topic was Pets.
"I want you all to work very hard because I
shall have a surprise for you soon,"
said Ms Miller.
"What is it, Miss?" asked Michael.
"A surprise, Michael, is a surprise,"
Ms Miller answered firmly.
Letang and Julie glanced at each other and
grinned.

Everyone had to choose a pet to write about. Rachel wanted to do
guinea-pigs because she had two of them at home. Sam chose dogs
because she had a new puppy.
"Can I do snakes, Miss?" asked Michael. "My dad's got one."
Some children wriggled and made faces but Ms Miller said "yes".

"I don't know what to do,"
sighed Julie.
"Nkoko my granny gave me a goat
when I was five," said Letang.
"My nan had a farm and she let me
feed her calves," said Julie.
Letang frowned. "But these books
don't have goats and calves."

4

"So what can we do?" asked Julie.
"I know!" replied Letang.
"We can look in the pet shop."
By home-time, the two girls had
made their plan.

5

On Saturday it was very cloudy and then it began raining hard. Letang and her dad waited inside the pet shop.

"It's pouring cats and dogs!" joked Letang's dad.

But Letang was worried. Would Julie still be able to come in the rain?

6

FANCY DOMESTIC RATS

"Siamese" Kittens

CHAPPY FOOD

DOG

0·0·65

Peanuts + bird seeds

FISH FOOD

Blackmoors   ANGEL FISH!   GUPPIES   GOLDFISH

DUTCH RABBITS

7

Suddenly the door swung open.
"We got caught in the rain!" laughed Julie's mum.
Letang liked the way she smiled a lot, even with drops of water falling from her hair and nose!

Letang and Julie began to look into the cages.
"Mum says I might get a pet when I'm older," said Julie.
"Mma says she doesn't like pets in cages," said Letang.

"Oh look here!" called Julie. "Fluffy pom-poms!"
Some tiny hamsters were tumbling all over each other.
"Oh mum!" complained Julie when her mum said it was time to go.
"Bye, hamsters!" whispered the girls before they left.

On Monday morning, Letang and Julie looked at the books on hamsters.

"That's the one!" said Letang.

"It's a Golden Hamster!"

The girls told Ms Miller about their visit to the pet shop and she seemed pleased.

"You two can work together on a hamster topic," she suggested.

All the children worked hard on their topic. Sometimes Julie's other teacher, Mr Carter, helped too.

A week later, Ms Miller came in
carrying a large cardboard box.
"Well, here's the surprise!" she said.
There were "oohs" and "aahs" as
slowly Ms Miller lifted out ...
a cage. Inside it was a little
golden hamster – just like
one from the pet shop!

Ms Miller and the class had a long talk. Each week two children would have to look after the hamster. Ms Miller looked at Letang and Julie.

"You two can be first!" she said. "But what shall we call it?"

Hammy

Puffy

Nibbles

Squeak

Nibbles

Every morning Letang and Julie hurried in to class to say hello to 'Nibbles'.

Letang and Julie wrote about Nibbles for their topic.

Our Class Pet

by Julie and Letang

We have a class pet.
We call him Nibbles.
He likes to nibble sunflower seeds
and then his cheeks puff out.
He wipes his whiskers with his paws.

Friday was clean-out day. Ms Miller offered to help.

"We must be careful not to frighten him," she said, gently getting hold of Nibbles and putting him into a deep box.

Letang and Julie changed the sawdust on the cage floor.

"Can I hold him for a little?" asked Letang.

"Keep your hands cupped," said Ms Miller. Carefully she placed Nibbles into Letang's hands with her own on top.

"He likes me!" giggled Letang. "You have a go, Julie!"

Julie shaped her hands like a nest. But as soon as Ms Miller put him in, Nibbles found a little hole and Julie's fingers couldn't move quickly enough to stop him. In a second he had jumped across her lap and was gone.

Everyone looked everywhere. The classroom was turned upside down.
When Mr Carter came in, he looked too.
"Perhaps Nibbles has found a secret little hide-out and will come back
for his dinner," said Mr Carter, trying to cheer Julie up.
The bell rang for playtime.
"Don't worry!" said Rachel to Letang and Julie.
"I'll show you the new game my sister taught me," said Sam.
But when they got outside, through the crowd in the corridor,
Julie wasn't there.

Letang found Julie crying in the cloakroom.
Michael had called her a nasty name and two
girls had whispered other bad things in her ear.
"Let's go and see Ms Miller," said Letang.

After play, Ms Miller spoke to the whole class. "We are all upset about Nibbles and if it is anyone's fault, it's mine. But I am much more upset that some of you are calling names to hurt someone. When I was little I was called "deafie" and it still hurts me now. So I want to know what we can do about this."

It was lunchtime before everyone had had their say.

At first, children from the class brought special titbits to leave overnight in Nibbles' cage. They hoped to find him there in the morning. But as the days went by and the cage stayed empty, most of them gave up. Only Letang and Julie still kept coming in early.

Then one morning they heard scratching.

"It's Nibbles!" whispered Julie. "He's going into his cage!"

"Quick!" said Letang.

Grabbing the string they had tied to the cage door, they gave it a sharp tug and the door swung down. Nibbles looked startled. He had been busy eating Michael's raisins!

The next day Class 3M had a party. The guest of honour
had to be kept locked up. But he was very well fed and ...
he was presented with a book all about himself!